10 LITTLE MONSTERS *visit* WASHINGTON

RICK WALTON

ILLUSTRATIONS BY
JESS SMART SMILEY

FAMILIUS

GREETINGS FROM

WASHINGTON

POST

To Gary Larson, who took us to
the Far Side so we could better
understand the Near Side.

—RW

For Jon, my favorite
part of Washington!

—JSS

Published by Familius™ LLC, www.familius.com

Familius books are available at special discounts for bulk purchases for sales promotions or for family
or corporate use. Special editions, including personalized covers, excerpts of existing books, or books
with corporate logos, can be created in large quantities for special needs. For more information, contact
Premium Sales at 559-876-2170 or email specialmarkets@familius.com.

Library of Congress Catalog-in-Publication Data
2015940072
ISBN 9781942672982

Printed in China

Book and jacket design by David Miles

10 9 8 7 6 5 4 3 2 1
First Edition

10 Little Monsters, looking for fun,
Take a trip to Washington.

10 Little Monsters, they can't wait
'Cause monsters love the Evergreen State!

10 Little Monsters, from park to park,
Travel the Trail of Lewis and Clark.

One monster says when they reach the sea,

"I'll see what's next.
How far can it be?"

The Lewis and Clark Trail runs for 3,700 miles, from Illinois to the mouth of the Columbia River. Follow the signs and you won't end up in the middle of the ocean.

9 Little Monsters, loaded with gear,
Start to hike up Mount Rainier.
They climb and they climb 'til they reach the top.
But one of the monsters forgets to stop.

Mt. Rainier is a volcano and the highest mountain in Washington. Thousands of people climb it every year. Most of them are smarter than monsters and stop when they reach the top.

Salmon are an important source of nutrition for Washington animals, plants, and people. Though leaping salmon are beautiful, don't you be a salmon. You are perfect just the way you are.

8 Little Monsters, just for fun,
Join the salmon on a run.
They swim up the river. They leap through the air—
'Til one is caught by a big brown bear.

Little Monsters find some ice.
Mmmm, it's cold. Mmmm, feels nice.
Someone says, "That one there."
One Little Monster flies through the air.

Pike Place Market is a huge public market where you can buy almost anything. If you want a fish, an employee will toss it to the counter for you to buy. Don't, however, expect an appliance store to toss the refrigerator of your choice.

CAUGHT THIS MORNING!

OVER NIGHT SHIPPING AVAILABLE!

$8.99 POUND LB

BUY ONE, GET ONE FREE!

FRESH!

FRESH

1.3 million people visit the observation deck of the 605-foot-tall Seattle Space Needle, which was built for the 1962 Seattle World's Fair. The smart visitors use the elevators.

6

Little Monsters *ahhh* and *oooh*.
One monster wants a better view.
That Little Monster climbs up higher.
ZAP! One monster catches fire.

5 Little Monsters can't stay dry
With all the rain clouds in the sky.
Happy monsters dance in the rain.

There goes a monster down the drain.

Rain falls in western Washington over 150 days a year.
That's a total of about 40 inches of rain, which is a lot,
but not enough to wash you down a drain, unless you are
a leaf . . . or a monster.

Little Monsters, off to San Juan,
Find the ferry and get right on.
One Little Monster makes a mistake.
One poor whale gets a bellyache.

The Washington Ferries carry 22 million passengers a year. Traveling by ferry is much more comfortable than traveling by whale.

3 Little Monsters say they hear
A long-lost relative lives near.
"Hey!" they call. "Where are you at?"
'Til a big foot falls and squashes one flat.

Many people claim to have seen Sasquatch, but no one has yet proved that he exists. If you want to visit long-lost relatives, you should first make sure they exist. And you should call them and tell them you're coming so they don't accidentally step on you.

2 Little Monsters, at Grand Coulee,
Learn how to make electricity.
One wants to see where the power goes.

The Grand Coulee Dam produces
enough power to run 2.3 million homes.
It's better for you to have the power
than for the power to have you.

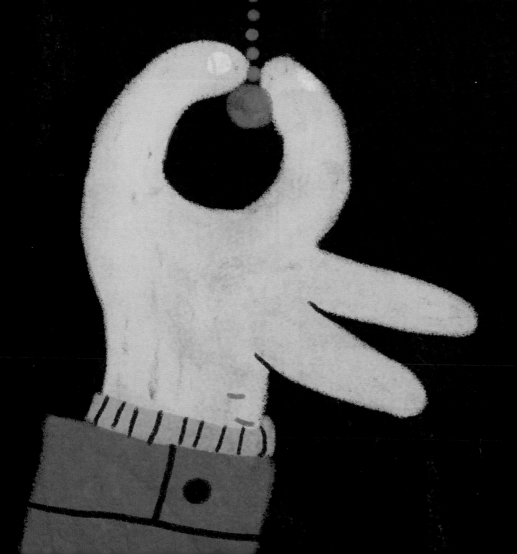

Oh, how bright the monster glows.

1 Little Monster asleep in a tree
With apples as far as the eye can see.
Along comes a young boy looking for lunch.
He reaches, he picks, takes a big bite, and . . .

About 3 out of every 5 apples grown
in the United States are grown in
Washington. All monsters are removed
before Washington apples are shipped
to your local store.